VANISHED INTO THIN AIR

The team leaned forward in their seats. Alex was so lucky to be up on the stage of a Broadway theater!

Slowly, the glass booth filled with fog. Alex's form wavered and disappeared. All anyone could see was clouds of fog. Then the fog slowly disappeared. The booth was empty!

The audience burst into applause. Finn looked down into the third row, straight at the team.

"Do you want your friend back?" he asked, waggling his eyebrows.

"You can keep him!" Gaby shouted jokingly.

"Oooo, the young lady says no," Finn said. "Should I listen to her, audience? Or should I bring Alex back from the sixth dimension?"

"Bring him back!" the audience yelled.

Slowly, the fog hissed into the booth. Soon, nobody could see anything. Then, once again, the fog began to disappear.

"And heeeeeere's Alex!" Finn cried, waving his arms.

But when the last of the fog cleared, the booth was empty!

Join the Team!

Do you watch GHOSTWRITER on PBS? Then you know that when you read and write to solve a mystery or unravel a puzzle, you're using the same smarts and skills the Ghostwriter team uses.

We hope you'll join the team and read along to help solve the mysterious and puzzling goings-on in these GHOSTWRITER books!

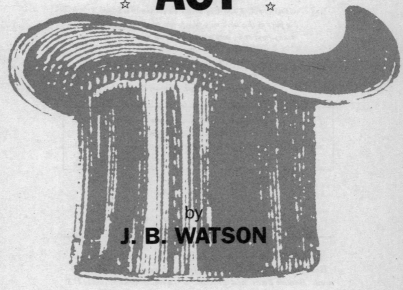

Ghost writer™

DISAPPEARING ACT

by
J. B. WATSON

ILLUSTRATIONS BY ERIC VELASQUEZ

A CHILDREN'S TELEVISION
WORKSHOP BOOK

BANTAM BOOKS

NEW YORK • TORONTO • LONDON • SYDNEY • AUCKLAND

DISAPPEARING ACT
A Bantam Book / April 1994

Ghostwriter, G**host**writer and ● are
trademarks of Children's Television Workshop.
All rights reserved. Used under authorization.

Cover design by Susan Herr
Interior illustrations by Eric Velasquez

ISBN 0-553-37308-0

Published simultaneously in the United States and Canada

Bantam Books are published by Bantam Books, a division of Bantam
Doubleday Dell Publishing Group, Inc. Its trademark, consisting of the
words "Bantam Books" and the portrayal of a rooster, is Registered in U.S.
Patent and Trademark Office and in other countries. Marca Registrada.
Bantam Books, 1540 Broadway, New York, New York 10036.

PRINTED IN THE UNITED STATES OF AMERICA

OPM   0   9   8   7   6   5   4   3   2   1

CHAPTER

☆ **1** ☆

"Move it or lose it, Alex," Gaby Fernandez told her older
brother. She stood impatiently in the doorway of their bed-
room and tapped the watch on her wrist. "We're supposed
to meet the team at one o'clock."

Alex laced up his high-tops with a sigh. "Gaby, I *know*
you decided to set your watch fifteen minutes fast so you
won't be late anymore. We have plenty of time."

"I did set it fifteen minutes fast," Gaby admitted. "But
then I forgot to wind it." She tossed Alex's denim jacket at
him. "Hurry up."

As Alex struggled into his jacket, Gaby took his elbow
and hustled him toward the front door. "Hey, watch out!"
Alex said as he crashed into a small table with a blue ceramic
vase. It was their mother's favorite.

Gaby reached out to steady it. It was lucky that her mother wasn't home. Both she and Gaby's father were in the front of the building, working in the family-owned Brooklyn bodega.

"I'm so excited," Gaby said, opening the front door. "I can't wait to see Sawchuck and Finn."

"For free," Alex added. "That's the best part."

Thanks to their friend Lenni Frazier, they were going to see the hottest ticket on Broadway. Harry Sawchuck and Riley Finn were magicians. They had been partners for years, then broke up in a public and bitter fight. Now they had reunited in a show called *The Battle of the World's Best Magicians*. Lenni's father, Max, was a jazz musician who was playing in the orchestra of the smash hit. He'd snagged tickets for Lenni and all her friends.

"Wait a second," Alex said, stopping in the doorway. "I want to make a sandwich to take with me. I'm starving."

"We don't have time," Gaby said, yanking him through the door.

Alex shut the door after them. He knew his sister well. Sometimes it was better to give in rather than listen to her complain for the next five hours.

"Now my stomach is going to rumble all through the show," Alex told her as they exited onto the street. "You won't be able to hear a thing, and it will serve you right."

Just then their friend Hector came out from the shadow of the building. He had been waiting for them. "You hungry, Alex? We can stop at a taco stand or something." Alex had met Hector when he'd volunteered to be part of a big brothers program. Hector had been shy at first, but now he and Alex were good friends.

"No, we can't," Gaby said. "We don't have time." She started to walk impatiently. She liked Hector, but ever since Alex had become his "big brother" she was always arguing with *two* people instead of *one*. Hector worshiped the sidewalks Alex's high-tops walked on. "You two drive me nuts," she muttered.

"Speaking of nuts, some trail mix would be nice," Alex said. Hector laughed as if it were the funniest thing he had ever heard.

Gaby rolled her eyes and walked faster. The subway station was only three blocks away. When they reached it, their friends Lenni, Jamal Jenkins, and Tina Nguyen were already waiting.

"Great, you're here!" Lenni greeted them. "I was starting to get worried."

"It's Alex's fault," Gaby said. "He took forever to get ready."

"She wouldn't even let me make a sandwich," Alex complained.

"You should have thought of it earlier," Gaby shot back.

"Alex, you can stop for a slice of pizza or something when we get to New York," Tina suggested.

"No way," Gaby said.

"Way," Alex said.

"Come on, Gaby," Tina said. "It would only take a minute."

"Alex only take a minute? Are you nuts?" Gaby grumbled. "He takes three hours to order a sandwich."

"Here comes the train!" Jamal said in a too-cheerful voice.

Nobody said much on the way to the theater. They'd looked forward to this Saturday matinee for weeks, but suddenly the mood was spoiled. As they got off the train in Manhattan and walked the few blocks to the theater, they were still quiet.

Above their heads, two men were tearing the sign off an old billboard. The sign read:

AF ER   THE TER
PLEASE MAK   MI
P Y R L A   D O   FE

Hector peered up at it. "What does it say?" he asked. "After the tree?"

"That doesn't make sense," Jamal said. He squinted at

the board. "I know. It used to say, 'After theater, please make mine Pyrlando Coffee.'"

"I know that brand," Alex said. "We sell it in the bodega. Three seventy-nine a can."

"Three sixty-five," Gaby said.

"No, three seventy-nine," Hector piped up.

"How do you know?" Gaby scoffed. "You've never stocked our shelves."

"Sure I did," Hector said. "Last Saturday I helped Alex."

"So *that's* how you got done so fast!" Gaby said to Alex furiously.

"Will you guys chill already?" Jamal said irritably.

Suddenly, the letters on the billboard over their heads started to glow. They rearranged themselves as they floated in the air. First they read: BE HAPPY. Then they read: BE A TEAM.

"Ghostwriter!" Tina exclaimed.

Ghostwriter was their mysterious friend. All anyone knew about him was that he had lived long ago, and he could communicate with them only through written words. He had revealed himself to Jamal first through his computer. Gradually, the other kids had begun to see his messages too. Now they all wore pens around their necks so that they could communicate with Ghostwriter whenever they wanted. Ghostwriter had made them into a team.

Everyone exchanged glances. They knew Ghostwriter was right. But it was hard to get *out* of a bad mood once you were in it, just because someone wanted you to. Even if it was Ghostwriter.

Lenni shrugged. "Well, if Ghostwriter can't cheer us up, maybe Sawchuck and Finn can."

They hurried the rest of the way to the theater. Max was waiting for them at the stage door. He gave them the tickets.

"Enjoy the show, gang," he said. "And remember, Lenni, I have to leave before the show's over to get to my next gig downtown. Make sure you go straight home, okay?"

"Okay, Dad," Lenni agreed. Just because Max was a musician didn't mean he didn't fuss over Lenni like any other parent.

They filed into the theater. A crowd milled in the lobby, and an excited buzz of conversation was in the air. Alex drifted closer to the refreshment bar. A nice big candy bar, he thought, would probably hold him until dinnertime.

"Can I help you?" the attendant asked.

"Sure," Alex said. "I'll have a . . . " He leaned over. "Four-fifty for a candy bar!"

The attendant gave a shrug. "That's entertainment!" he said.

"I call it a rip-off," Alex said. But he grinned to let the guy know he didn't blame him.

The attendant glanced around quickly and leaned toward Alex. "Try the peanut vendor outside," he murmured. "You can get a bag for fifty cents."

"Thanks," Alex said gratefully. Gaby and the rest of the team were just getting their programs from an usher. He hurried over. "I'm going outside to get some peanuts."

"Don't be long," Lenni advised him.

Alex hurried outside. He spotted the vendor's cart by the stage entrance. Written on the side of the yellow cart in bright red letters was:

WYLIE'S PEANUTS
THEY'RE FRESH! 50¢

Alex hurried over. He dug into the pocket of his jeans and found two quarters. The vendor handed him a warm paper bag. Alex was just about to reach into the bag for the first roasted peanut when he saw the stage door open right next to him. A tall, husky man stormed out, followed by a short, slender man with a ponytail. They were dressed in ugly polyester tuxedos with wide lapels piped in contrasting colors. The slender man's ruffled shirt was lime-green. The other's was lavender.

Alex recognized them right away. They were the stars

of the show, Harry Sawchuck and Riley Finn. They called their costumes "Las Vegas chic."

Alex couldn't believe it. Maybe he could get their autographs. He had his Ghostwriter team pen around his neck. Sawchuck and Finn could write on the peanut bag. Gaby would turn as green as Riley Finn's shirt!

He started toward the pair, but then he realized that Sawchuck and Finn were fighting. They'd always been reported as having a stormy partnership. But when this show was announced, they appeared together for publicity and said that their troubles were history.

But it looked like all the good feelings were only for the television cameras. Harry Sawchuck leaned over Riley Finn and shook his finger in his face. The tall, muscular man towered over Finn.

"Don't you try any funny business with me!" Sawchuck hissed.

"How would you know what funny business is, Harry?" Finn said. "You'd have to have a sense of humor."

"Don't get cute with me," Harry Sawchuck said furiously. "You were nobody when I found you. You were playing birthday parties and living in a dump. I taught you everything you know!"

"And then I had to unlearn it!" Finn shot back.

Alex wondered if he should move away. Sawchuck and

Finn hadn't seen him yet. But if they did, they might think that he was eavesdropping. Of course, he *was*.

Suddenly, Sawchuck grabbed Finn's frilly shirtfront. His face looked as red as a tomato against his lavender shirt. "You'd better shut your face, Finn!" he bellowed. "I've had it. If you don't watch it, I'm going to wreck your career!"

CHAPTER

☆ **2** ☆

Alex stepped back. There was a murderous gleam in Harry Sawchuck's eyes. Even though the gleam wasn't directed at Alex, it was scary.

Suddenly, the stage door opened, and a woman in a shocking-pink satin dress stuck her head out. She was blond and pretty. "Are you two fighting again?"

"He started it!" Finn said.

"It was his fault!" Sawchuck sputtered.

"Enough already!" the woman snapped.

The two men looked sheepish. "Sorry, Galina," Finn said.

"He just makes me so *mad,*" Sawchuck said.

"Get in here," Galina said sternly. "You've got five minutes until curtain."

Sawchuck and Finn started to file past Galina. Alex breathed a sigh of relief. Nobody had noticed him.

Suddenly, Gaby came running out from the front of the theater. "Alex!" she shouted. "Hurry up! Just because our tickets are free doesn't mean you can be late!"

The two magicians and Galina turned and stared at him. This wasn't the first time that Alex wished his sister were the shy, soft-spoken type. Now the adults knew that he had overheard Sawchuck and Finn arguing!

"We have great seats!" Gaby called. "Third row center!"

Alex dashed toward the theater doors. He tried to catch up with Gaby, but his sister was already heading across the lobby. She beckoned for him to hurry up.

"Gaby, wait up!" Alex said in a stage whisper. He quickened his pace and almost ran into a stocky boy about his own age wearing a blue suit and a red tie. The boy was standing next to a middle-aged, bearlike man with a bald head.

"Oops, sorry," Alex apologized.

Instead of smiling or saying it was all right, the boy gave him a haughty look. The man took the boy's arm and moved him away. Then the pair pushed past Alex and started down the aisle.

"Well, excuse *me*," Alex muttered.

The boy and his bald companion walked to the third row just ahead of Alex and began climbing over people's feet

☆ **13** ☆

as they pushed toward their seats. People said "ouch!" and shot them nasty looks, but the pair ignored everyone. They settled into two seats next to Jamal.

Alex started down the row, trying to avoid everyone's feet. He looked ahead and saw Jamal arguing with the haughty boy.

"It's my friend's seat," Jamal said.

"I think not," the boy said. He folded his plump hands in his lap.

"Now, hold on," Jamal said, frustrated. "Why don't you at least show me your ticket?"

"*Me* show *you* my ticket?" the boy asked. "I think *not*."

"Oh, yeah?" Jamal asked. "I think *so*."

"You mustn't speak to his imper . . . Alexis that way," the bald man said in a low voice.

"Well, don't take my friend's seat," Jamal said stubbornly.

"Hold on, everyone," Alex said. He held out his ticket stub. "See? I'm in seat six."

The boy ignored him. But the bald man took the stub and looked at it. He sighed. He pulled out his ticket stubs. Then he looked down at the seats. "You're right, young man." he said. "Our seats are next to yours. Our apologies. Alexis, move to this side, please."

"Anyone can make a mistake," Alex said, wanting to be friendly.

☆ **14** ☆

The boy let out a big sigh, as though it were Alex's fault that he had to move. He slipped into the seat on the opposite side of the bald man, and Alex sat down.

Alex leaned over. "My name is Alex too."

The boy looked over. "My name is Alexis. Not Alex."

"It's close," Alex said. "Would either of you like a peanut?" He held out the bag and shook it so that the fresh-roasted smell wafted up.

The boy looked tempted. "Well . . . maybe one."

But Alexis's companion put his hand over the bag. "No, Alexis," he said firmly. "These are from the street. Wait to eat until we get back to Little Odessa."

Alexis pushed the peanuts back at Alex.

Alex shrugged and turned to Jamal. So much for trying to be friendly. Then he remembered what he'd overheard. "Hey, I heard Sawchuck and Finn arguing," he whispered to Jamal. "They aren't friends at all. They're enemies!"

Jamal looked skeptical. "Maybe they were rehearsing." Sawchuck and Finn had always used their rivalry as comic relief in their act.

"No, it's for real," Alex insisted. "Sawchuck told Finn that he'd ruin his career!"

Lenni leaned over. "Shhhh. The musicians are tuning up. They're going to start soon."

"Why are they down in that hole?" Gaby asked, craning

her neck. This was her first Broadway play, and she wanted to know everything.

Lenni smiled. "It's called the orchestra pit," she said. Just then, the lights in the theater slowly went down. "Those are called the *house lights*," Lenni explained. "That means the show is about to start."

"Lenni, shush," Tina said good-naturedly. "The curtain is going up."

"I'm going to figure out all the tricks," Lenni said, leaning forward.

"Me, too," Gaby said. "It'll be a cinch."

"Dream on," Alex said. "Do you really think you're smarter than Sawchuck and Finn?"

Gaby grinned. "Do you really want me to answer that?"

"Shhh," Tina said. She leaned forward excitedly as Sawchuck walked to center stage and waited for the applause to die down. He looked upset. The stage was completely dark and empty except for spotlights on the magician and on one large white garbage can pushed to the edge of the stage near the back. There were no props; there was no stage set at all. The audience quieted, sensing something was wrong.

"The sides of the stage are called the *wings*," Lenni whispered to Gaby. Tina looked at her, exasperated. Lenni grinned. "Sorry."

Harry Sawchuck's lavender shirt glowed against the darkness. "Good evening, ladies and gentleman, children, magic lovers everywhere," he said in a low, shaky voice. "I have tragic news for you this afternoon. Tragic news for the community of magicians, and the world at large. Sawchuck and Finn cannot go on."

The audience began to murmur. Alex nudged Jamal. He'd *told* him something was wrong.

"Riley Finn is dead," Harry Sawchuck said.

CHAPTER

☆ **3** ☆

The audience gasped. Tina's hands flew to her mouth. "Oh, *no*!" she cried.

"Your money will be refunded, of course," Harry Sawchuck said. He stepped a little closer to the audience. "You know, Riley always said that he would be able to cheat death. He said he'd give me a message from the other side. Well, I guess even the second greatest magician in the world couldn't do it."

The audience gasped again. But this time, it was because behind Harry Sawchuck, the garbage can was slowly rising in the air. It floated eerily above the stage, coming closer and closer to Sawchuck.

"I'll miss Riley Finn," Sawchuck said. "He was my friend as well as my colleague."

The audience started to murmur. By now they suspected that Riley Finn's "death" was part of the act. The audience began to laugh as the garbage can tilted over Harry Sawchuck's head.

Sawchuck frowned and spoke louder. "We were like this." He held up two entwined fingers. "So if you can hear me, little buddy," he said, almost sobbing, "I miss you!"

Suddenly, the can tipped over. Banana peels, apple cores, and discarded frozen-food boxes were upended over Harry Sawchuck's head. The audience burst out laughing.

Sawchuck yelped and jumped away. He wiped his face with his handkerchief. He peered into the blackness. "Riley?"

An eerie light suddenly illuminated a coffin that was standing upright at the back of the stage. The top slowly creaked open to reveal Riley Finn. He was wrapped in a white sheet, and his eyes were closed.

"Little buddy?" Sawchuck squeaked.

Slowly, the body of Riley Finn disappeared. A skeleton took its place.

Tina gasped, leaning so far forward that she almost knocked off the beret of the woman in front of her.

The skeleton slowly disappeared, and Riley Finn appeared again. He opened his eyes.

Harry Sawchuck screamed. He ran into the audience and

up the aisle. Riley Finn stared with blank, unseeing eyes. Even though everybody knew it was a trick, it was spooky.

Sawchuck picked out a man in the audience. "You've got to help me," he babbled. "I swear I didn't arrange this. Could you go up on the stage and check it out? Riley wouldn't hurt you. He loved his fans."

At the challenge, the man got up and went down the aisle nervously. He stepped up onto the stage and went toward the coffin. While everyone had been watching Sawchuck, Finn had disappeared again. Now the coffin was empty.

"Check it out," Sawchuck urged. "You'll be fine. I promise. I'll be right here."

Slowly, the man climbed into the coffin. The audience gasped as he slowly disappeared.

"Oh, my gosh!" Sawchuck screamed. "I lost another one!"

He ran toward the stage. As he mounted the steps, Riley Finn came running out from the wings.

"Did you lose him?" he shrieked. They both ran to the coffin. Slowly, the man reappeared. They both reached in and hauled him out.

The audience burst into applause, and the audience volunteer took a bow.

"I wish he had picked me," Gaby said enviously.

"That was incredible," Tina said. "How did they do it?"

"It was a trick," Lenni said.

Jamal's mouth twisted into a half grin. "Great deduction, Lenni."

Everyone's attention turned back to the stage when Riley Finn pulled a white dove out of the air and made it disappear.

For the next hour and a half, the team was spellbound by the incredible tricks of Sawchuck and Finn. They pulled objects out of the air. They correctly guessed what audience members had in their pockets. Sawchuck escaped from a mailbag inside a garbage Dumpster, and Finn levitated so high off the stage that they couldn't see him anymore.

Finally, the curtain opened on the last trick. On the right side of the eerily darkened stage was a folding screen that surrounded a table on three sides. Underneath the table were two candelabras, and on top of it was a large glass booth about the size of a refrigerator.

Riley Finn came out of the wings. He stood on the edge of the stage, close to the audience. "As you can see, there is nothing underneath the table besides the candelabras," he said. "And the booth is transparent. And now, I need a volunteer from the audience."

Hector's and Gaby's hands shot up immediately. Jamal's did too. A moment later Tina raised her hand. Jamal poked Alex, and he raised his hand slowly. On the other side of the bald man, the boy Alexis started to raise his hand, but the man shook his head and Alexis lowered it.

Galina came out of the wings from the other side of the stage. "Galina," Finn said, "will you choose my victim—I mean, volunteer?"

Galina walked down the aisle. She walked past them, and Gaby slumped down in disappointment. Jamal lowered his hand. But Alex kept his absentmindedly in the air.

Galina turned back. Her eyes roamed over the third row. Then she pointed straight at Alex. "I have a volunteer!"

Alex shot up from his seat in surprise. "No fair," Gaby muttered as he inched past the other people in the row.

Galina took Alex's hand in hers. She led him down the aisle and up the side stairs to the wings. A moment later, Alex came out from behind the curtains at the rear of the stage.

While Galina tied Alex's hands behind him with a silk scarf, Finn asked Alex his name. "Well, Alex," he said, "you're a very brave young man. I wouldn't trust me if I were you."

Alex laughed along with the audience. Galina slipped a black velvet hood over his head. "Too late now, son," Finn said. "Galina, please lead our volunteer to the booth."

Galina helped Alex up on the table and into the booth. She shut the door firmly.

"Now, watch carefully, ladies and gentlemen," Riley Finn said. "The booth is a key to the sixth dimension. Alex will now visit it—whether he wants to or not."

The team leaned forward in their seats. Alex was so lucky to be up on the stage of a Broadway theater!

Slowly, the glass booth filled with fog. Alex's form wavered and disappeared. All anyone could see was clouds of fog. Then the fog slowly disappeared. The booth was empty!

The audience burst into applause. Finn looked down into the third row, straight at the team.

"Do you want your friend back?" he asked, waggling his eyebrows.

"You can keep him!" Gaby shouted jokingly.

"Oooo, the young lady says no," Finn said. "Should I listen to her, audience? Or should I bring Alex back from the sixth dimension?"

"Bring him back!" the audience yelled.

"Are you *sure*?" Finn said.

"Yes!" The audience answered.

Finn cupped a hand behind his ear. "Are you *positive*? He looked like a nasty little fellow to me."

"YES!" the audience roared. By now, everyone was laughing.

Slowly, the fog hissed into the booth. Soon, nobody

could see anything. Then, once again, the fog began to disappear.

"And heeeeeere's Alex!" Finn cried, waving his arms.

But when the last of the fog cleared, the booth was empty!

CHAPTER

☆ **4** ☆

The audience burst into laughter and applause. Riley Finn looked startled. Then he smiled nervously.

"I guess we lost another one!" he said, and the audience laughed even louder. They burst into applause as Sawchuck, Finn, and Galina took their final bows.

The curtains swept closed, and Tina turned to Jamal. "That was the funniest ending ever!" she said. "Sawchuck and Finn are so good that they can *pretend* to mess up a trick."

The boy and the bald man got up to go. "Did you enjoy the show, Alexis?" the bald man asked.

"It was all right," Alexis said with a sniff. "I prefer the magicians in Europe."

Jamal pressed the tip of his nose upward with his

index finger to show the rest of the team his opinion of Alexis: the kid was a major snob. A giggle ran from Tina all the way down the team and ended in a muffled snort from Hector.

"Hurry up, Alexis," the bald man urged. "We must catch the D train. I have to get to work." The two filed out to the aisle.

"I wonder where Alex went during the trick?" Jamal said. "That box probably has a door in back."

"But it was made of glass!" Tina said. "If there had been a door, we would have seen it."

"Alex can tell us for sure how they did it," Lenni said.

"Right," Gaby agreed.

But where was Alex? Five minutes passed, then ten. Everyone was getting impatient.

"That Alex," Gaby grumbled. "Maybe he's pulling a *real* disappearing act just to be funny."

"Maybe he's talking to Sawchuck and Finn," Tina said excitedly.

"He's probably getting their autographs," Lenni said enviously.

Just then the team noticed Galina heading down the aisle toward them. She had scrubbed off her stage makeup, and was wearing a sweatshirt and jeans. "Excuse me. Are you waiting for Alex?"

"We're his friends," Lenni said.

"Mr. Sawchuck and Mr. Finn would like to see you," Galina said. "Follow me, please."

Walking quickly, Galina led them up to the stage and into the wings.

"I bet Alex asked Sawchuck and Finn if they'd sign all of our programs too," Gaby whispered to Tina. "He's the best brother."

"You didn't think so this morning," Tina reminded her.

Galina led them backstage. Props from the show were still lying around. Birds in cages twittered. A stagehand was rolling a huge mirror to the side. The Dumpster Sawchuck had escaped from sat waiting for the next performance.

They followed Galina to a staircase. They climbed up in single file and came to a door at the top. Galina knocked and opened it.

Harry Sawchuck and Riley Finn smiled. "Hello, fans," said Sawchuck.

"Hi! Where's Alex?" Gaby asked, looking around.

Sawchuck looked at Galina. "Thank you, Galina. That's enough for now." After Galina had left and shut the door, he said in an undertone to Finn, "No sense letting her know more than she does already."

"Know what?" Jamal asked.

"Where's Alex?" Gaby asked.

"Actually . . . " Sawchuck said nervously,

"As a matter of fact . . . " Finn said. His gaze roamed

over the team's questioning faces. "I'm sorry, kids," he said. "I don't know how it happened. But we seem to have lost your friend."

"What do you mean, you lost our friend?" Jamal demanded.

"How could you *lose* him?" Tina asked.

"Where's my brother?" Gaby demanded.

"Look, why don't we all sit down," Sawchuck said soothingly.

"I don't want to sit down!" Gaby cried. "I want my brother!"

"Please tell us what happened," Jamal said.

Riley ran his hands through his hair. Wisps stuck out from his ponytail. "Okay. Curtain up, my entrance. Booth is stage right. Galina gets volunteer, puts him in the booth. The fog comes up. He disappears. Poof, sha-zam, no problem. Only when he was supposed to come *back,* he didn't."

"Where did he go?" Jamal asked impatiently. "I mean, where was he *supposed* to go?"

"We can't tell him how the trick worked," Sawchuck muttered to Riley. "Magician's code of honor, you know."

Jamal's dark eyes glittered. "Maybe you'd like to tell the *police* how the trick was supposed to work."

Sawchuck tugged at his collar. "Ah, now, no need for that, no need. I'm sure your friend is just playing a trick on us. People do it all the time, try to stump the magicians and all that."

The team hesitated. Maybe Alex *was* playing a trick on them. If he was, it was his best ever.

"Maybe he's paying me back for getting on his case this morning," Gaby murmured to Tina.

Sawchuck overheard her. He smiled broadly. "You see? Your friend is very clever. When we find him, we should hire him for our show!" Finn and Sawchuck laughed a bit too loudly.

"So, leave it to us," Sawchuck continued. "We'll find him. If you'll follow us to the stage, we'll show you how the trick works. And let's hold off on calling the police for now. Agreed?"

The team exchanged glances. "Agreed," Gaby said.

"For now," Jamal added.

Sawchuck looked relieved. "But let's keep this between ourselves, okay? Don't even tell Galina. She thinks that one of us is playing a practical joke on the other and that Alex is part of it."

"She thinks we're a couple of overgrown kids," Finn said.

"When it comes to you, I wouldn't say *overgrown,*" Sawchuck said, looking down at Finn.

"At least I have a developed *brain,*" Finn shot back.

"*Is* one of you playing a practical joke?" Tina asked.

"Not *me,*" Finn declared. "I swear."

"I would never be so immature," Sawchuck said, opening the door. Galina was standing right outside. "What are you doing?" he barked.

"I was coming to get you," Galina said wildly. "The animals got out of their cages! I'm afraid the rabbits will eat the birds."

"Rabbits don't eat birds, Galina," Sawchuck said. "We've been over that."

"Well, these creatures are all over my dressing room!" Galina cried. "I'm afraid of those rabbits!" She looked at Riley Finn. "They're yours. You have to catch them."

Finn sighed. "All right. Go ahead, Harry. I'll catch up."

Everyone trooped back through the wings to the stage. The booth sat on the left side of the stage, where it had been during the trick. Sawchuck led them to it.

Jamal bent down and looked under the table. "Hey, there's a platform back there."

"Why didn't we see it during the show?" Lenni asked.

"Because of mirrors," Sawchuck explained. "See? They're reflecting the screen back at you. The angle makes it look like the space underneath the table is empty. The table only has two legs, not four. Two of the legs are just reflections. And there's only one candelabra underneath, not two."

"So it *looks* like there's empty space underneath the table all the way back to the screen, but there isn't," Jamal said.

"Exactly. The mirrors form the sides of that triangle-shaped compartment behind the table. You can't see it because the mirrors reflect the screen and the table legs and candelabra. Part of the disappearing booth rests on the secret compartment. When the fog enters the booth, Galina goes around the screen—everyone is looking at Finn at that point—and unhinges the little door. Alex climbs into the secret compartment and waits. When Galina comes back and signals him, he climbs back into the booth. Simple. We've done it a thousand times. Only this time, Galina says that when she opened the back of the box—the opening is behind the screen—Alex wasn't there."

"Didn't Galina look for Alex?" Tina asked.

Sawchuck nodded. "She couldn't find him anywhere backstage. But the show must go on. Galina figured that Riley had done something different with the trick and forgot to tell her."

Jamal crawled into the secret compartment and poked his head out. "There's no way out except backstage. Are you telling us that *nobody* saw Alex?"

"Nobody. I asked all the stagehands," Sawchuck said. "Listen, kids, I want to check on the rabbits," he added. "At the last theater we were in, the cleaning bill was huge. Be right back. Don't worry now. He'll probably show up and laugh in our faces."

He walked off the stage. Jamal climbed out of the compartment and joined the others.

"I don't know about you guys," Gaby said. "But I'm not sure that even Alex would keep us in suspense this long. I think he might really be missing." Her voice sounded a little wobbly.

"What are we going to do?" Tina wondered.

"Do you think we should call the police?" Lenni asked. "Gaby's right. This feels kind of spooky. Alex disappeared into thin air."

"But what if Alex *is* playing a trick?" Hector asked. "We could get him in big trouble."

"Wouldn't the police call my parents?" Gaby asked. "They'd flip out if they knew Alex was missing. They wouldn't let us out of the house for fifty years."

"Sawchuck and Finn said they could find him," Lenni said. But she didn't sound very positive.

"All they've done is argue and try to catch rabbits," Tina said gloomily.

Jamal looked at them. "Okay, team," he said. "I think we should try to figure out what happened to Alex by ourselves."

Tina nodded. "But if we can't, and he doesn't come back, then we call the police."

"Agreed?" Jamal asked, and everyone nodded.

"I know one thing," Gaby said. "I can't wait to find Alex. Because when I do, I'm going to kill him!"

"Okay, where should we start?" Tina asked.

"The first step is to get organized," Jamal said.

"Right," Lenni agreed. "Let's start a casebook." She reached into her backpack and brought out her notebook. Turning to a blank page, she wrote CASEBOOK across the top.

"There are two questions we have to answer," Jamal said. "Number one: Why did Alex disappear? And number two: Where is he?"

Lenni wrote down in the casebook *Why did Alex disappear?* Then she wrote *Where is Alex?*

Suddenly, the question WHERE IS ALEX began to blink insistently. "Ghostwriter knows something's wrong," Lenni said.

"Let's ask him if he can read anything around Alex,"

Tina suggested. Ghostwriter couldn't see people or forms, but he could read. If there was anything with words around Alex, it could be a clue.

Lenni wrote GHOSTWRITER, ALEX IS MISSING. CAN YOU READ ANYTHING NEAR HIM?

Ghostwriter zipped off. In a moment, he was back. Words appeared on the casebook page. OTIS 12345.

It was the team's first clue. But what did it mean? Lenni turned to a fresh sheet in the casebook and wrote *Evidence* at the top. She wrote OTIS 12345 underneath it.

Jamal snapped his fingers. "I just remembered. Alex told me before the show that he overheard Sawchuck and Finn arguing. He said that Sawchuck threatened to ruin Finn's career."

"So maybe he messed up Finn's trick," Tina said. "Let's put Harry Sawchuck down on our list of suspects."

Lenni turned to another page and wrote *Suspects* on top. She wrote down Sawchuck's name.

"What about Riley Finn?" Hector asked. "He could have done it to sabotage the show, to get Harry back for threatening him."

Lenni wrote down the other magician's name.

Suddenly, Tina looked scared. "Or what if Sawchuck *knew* that Alex overheard the threat and wanted to get rid of him?"

Suddenly, tears started to slip down Gaby's face. It had hit her that Alex's disappearance could be serious.

"Don't worry, Gaby," Jamal said gently. "We'll find him."

"It isn't just that. I was so mean to Alex this morning," Gaby said. "And I told Riley Finn not to bring him back. And I just remembered something else. Before the show, I ran out and yelled at Alex to hurry. Sawchuck and Finn noticed Alex then. They *did* know he overheard them—because of me! Now he's probably in danger and it's all my fault!"

At first, Alex had thought that his disappearance was part of the trick. When the fog filled the box, the floor had suddenly opened underneath his feet. He'd fallen down a long chute and landed on what felt like an old mattress. He had sat there, waiting. He'd heard the laughter and applause above him. He waited for someone to come and lead him up to the stage.

It seemed like forever until he heard footsteps coming down stairs. He'd asked the person what was going on, and got no answer.

The person picked him up. Relieved, Alex figured that the person was bringing him back to the stage. The arms held him tightly and were very strong. With the hood still on his head, he couldn't see a thing. He concentrated on sounds.

He heard a whoosh. Then a whirr. His stomach lurched. He was moving. An elevator! He couldn't tell if it was going up or down. Suddenly, Alex felt scared. He knew this wasn't part of the trick. Something was wrong. Very wrong.

Alex pushed against the hard chest. He yelled and tried to punch, even though his wrists were tied together. The massive arms squeezed him, tighter and tighter, until he could barely breathe. Alex stopped struggling.

The whirr stopped. Alex heard another whoosh. The elevator doors must have opened. He was carried for a few seconds. Then he recognized the clunk of a metal bar being pushed. He heard a heavy door open, then shut. Cool air moved against him. He was outside!

He heard the faint sound of car horns. He must be near the street. Alex began to struggle again. "Help!" he shouted. "Help!" His voice came out muffled because of the hood. The huge arms tightened again, and Alex stopped yelling.

Crunch, crunch, crunch. Footsteps against something—loose stones or gravel.

Clang, clang, clang. Metal stairs! Alex felt himself being carried up, up. He felt the man's leg swing over something. Then the other leg.

Chink, chink, chink. Down this time, in an unsteady

way, the man clasping Alex tightly to his chest. The air smelled swampy. Suddenly, Alex was dumped on the floor.

Finally, the man spoke. "There you go, right where you belong." The man spoke in an accent Alex couldn't place. He said another word, a foreign word. It sounded like *zaarveech*.

Chink, chink, chink. The man was leaving! "Hey!" Alex yelled. "What's happening?" No answer.

Alex slowly began moving his wrists back and forth. Gradually he managed to unloosen the knot in the silk scarf. At last he slipped his hands free.

Alex whipped off the hood and looked around. He was in a dark, round wooden room. There was no roof, just a circle of gray sky above. He was just in time to see a metal chain ladder disappear over the edge of the wall.

"Hey!" he shouted. "Hey! Come back!"

But he heard the man climbing down the stairs on the other side. No one else could hear him. No one would come.

He gazed around. The walls were dark wood, but they were smooth. There were no footholds anywhere. He was trapped!

Alex reached for the Ghostwriter pen around his neck. If he could find something to write on, he could send a message to the team. But his pen was missing! It must have fallen off.

Alex felt his pockets and pulled out the bag of peanuts he'd bought earlier. Without a pen or pencil, he couldn't use the bag to write on.

Suddenly, the letters began to move. They rose off the package and hung in the air.

WYLIE'S PEANUTS
THEY'RE FRESH 50¢

The letters and the zero from 50 turned into:

WHERE ARE YOU

Alex hit the floor in frustration. He couldn't write back! He didn't have a thing to write with. But then, suddenly, he had an idea. He *did* have something he could use.

Attention, Reader
Can you figure out how Alex can send a message to the team?
—Ghostwriter

The team huddled in a tight circle on the bare stage. They spoke in whispers. The theater was now a little spooky with just stage lights and no activity.

Jamal looked over Lenni's shoulder. "Did Ghostwriter bring back a message yet?"

"Not yet," Lenni said.

Then, there it was. MESSAGE FROM ALEX: ?

"A question mark," Tina said, disappointed. "Alex doesn't know where he is."

Gaby took the casebook from Lenni's hands. She wrote: HOW IS ALEX?

Moments ticked by. Ghostwriter didn't answer.

"Oh, no!" Gaby wailed. "There's something wrong, I just know it!" She started to cry again.

"Wait," Jamal said. "Look."

MESSAGE FROM ALEX: OK.

"You see, Gaby? He's fine," Jamal said. "And none of this is your fault, either. Now let's ask Ghostwriter to find out if Alex is close by."

Lenni wrote out the question to Ghostwriter and they waited for the answer.

"Why is it taking so long?" Hector asked.

"I don't know," Jamal said worriedly.

After a moment, the message came back. YES.

"What should we ask next?" Gaby asked.

"Ask Alex to describe where he's being held," Tina suggested.

Alex sat, staring at the peanut bag. The letters began to glow again. They spelled PICTURE. Alex frowned. Ghostwriter didn't have many letters to work with. But what was he trying to ask him? He thought a minute. Ghostwriter must want him to describe his surroundings. But Alex didn't have a way to form so many letters. He had to get across one main idea. He was in a round space. Using the peanuts, he sent the only message he could.

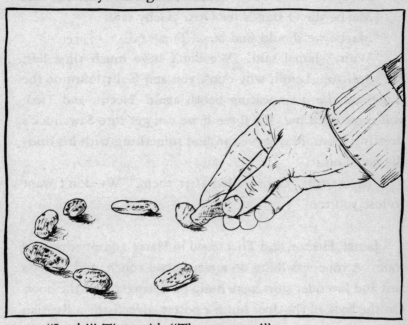

"Look!" Tina said. "The message!"

They all stared at the notebook page, puzzled. "It's just an O," Gaby said. "What does it mean?"

"Maybe it has to do with Otis," Lenni suggested. "Whoever he is."

Suddenly, Jamal snapped his fingers and pointed to the far wall. There was a poster advertising the show. Bright green letters spelled out *THE BATTLE OF THE WORLD'S*

BEST MAGICIANS: HARRY O. SAWCHUCK AND RILEY FINN.

"Harry O. Sawchuck!" Lenni exclaimed.

"Maybe the O stands for Otis," Gaby said.

"Maybe we should find out," Tina said.

"Wait," Jamal said. "We don't have much time left. Let's split up. Lenni, why don't you and Gaby examine the stage and the disappearing booth again. Hector and Tina, you come with me. We'll see if we can get into Sawchuck's dressing room. Maybe we can find something with his middle name on it."

"Be careful!" Gaby called after them. "We don't want to lose you too!"

Jamal, Hector, and Tina stood in Harry's empty dressing room. A robe was flung on a ratty plaid couch, and Harry's suit and lavender shirt were hung on a hanger near the door. On the back of the door hung a poster advertising a Russian circus.

"Okay," Jamal said. "Let's start."

Tina looked through Harry's dressing table. Photographs were stuck into the mirror frame, and Tina bent closer to look at them. One of them was a black-and-white photograph. A young boy stood next to a stout older woman. He had the same broad jaw and wide nose as Harry Sawchuck. Behind them was a sign with strange letters Tina didn't recognize.

Tina went back to searching the dressing table. There was a pile of bills on one corner. Next to it was a checkbook. She flipped it open. Printed on the check was HARRY OMAR SAWCHUCK.

Tina sighed. "Look, guys," she said, holding out the checkbook. "Harry isn't an Otis. He's an Omar."

"Too bad," Jamal said. "But that doesn't let him off the hook."

Suddenly, the letters on the poster on the back of Harry's door began to glow and float. They spelled: BEWARE OF . . .

Other letters flew over from around the room, starting to spell another word. F . . . A . . . L . . .

But suddenly, the door burst open. Galina stood in the doorway.

"You!" she cried, pointing at them. "Come with me!"

CHAPTER

☆ 6 ☆

Tina backed up into the dressing table with a clatter. "We weren't doing anything," she said.

"We just—" Jamal started.

"Come with me," Galina ordered, and started to walk out.

Tina, Jamal, and Hector exchanged questioning looks. Was Galina going to lead them to Harry Sawchuck? Would he "disappear" them too?

"Come!" Galina called from the hall. "Your friends are waiting. They asked me to find you."

"Whew," Tina said, blowing out a breath.

They followed Galina to the stage. Gaby and Lenni were standing by the disappearing booth.

"Galina found you," Lenni said. "Good. We wanted you to see this." Her face was anxious.

A big knife stuck out of the wooden screen around the box. A piece of paper fluttered from it. Jamal, Tina, and Hector looked closer. It was a note that read:

Beware of false princes. Give up your claims. There is only one prince. Long live the czarevitch. No police.

"Ghostwriter tried to tell us about this!" Tina murmured.

"Alex really *has* been kidnapped," Jamal said.

"What's this?" Harry Sawchuck's voice boomed out as he strode onto the stage. He leaned over. "This is a circus knife," he said. "It's used in knife-throwing acts. Right, Galina?"

Galina examined the knife, then shrugged. "Maybe."

"What's this—a note?" Sawchuck asked. Jamal noticed that he gave a little jump when he was almost finished reading. His face turned pale. "Th-this is outrageous," he stammered.

"Do you know anything about this note?" Lenni asked.

"Of course not!" Sawchuck thundered.

"Were you ever in the circus, Mr. Sawchuck?" Tina asked. "Is that why you recognized the knife?"

"I started in the circus," Sawchuck said.

Jamal turned to Galina. "Galina, what happened when you didn't find Alex in the box?"

"I was surprised," Galina said. "I thought that maybe Harry and Riley had changed the trick and forgot to tell me, or that Alex had slipped past me in the dark and was trying to turn the tables on the magicians. So I just waited."

"And what were you doing when the trick was going on?" Lenni asked Harry Sawchuck.

"I was backstage, having a glass of tea," Sawchuck said. "I never watch Riley's tricks. Why should I? It's not like I could *learn* something."

Jamal studied the note. "This really changes things," he said. "If we call the police, we could be putting Alex in danger."

"Exactly my thought," Sawchuck said. "No police. I have to call my publicist. Galina, come with me. Kids, we'll be up in our dressing rooms. We need to figure out how to handle this with the press."

"Gee, thanks for the help," Lenni murmured as soon as Sawchuck and Galina were out of earshot.

Hector was staring at the note. "What's a cizaar—ee—vitch?" he asked.

"I know the word czar," Lenni said, pronouncing it *zar*. "That's what the king of Russia was called a long time ago, before the Communists took over during the Russian Revolution."

"Then what's a czarevitch?" Gaby asked.

Lenni shook her head. "I don't know."

Tina flipped open the casebook and entered the circus knife and *czarevitch?* under *Evidence.* "Why is it in Alex's kidnapping note?" she wondered, aloud. "Wasn't the Russian Revolution a super long time ago?"

"I think about seventy years ago," Lenni said.

The words in the casebook began to rearrange. "Wait," Tina said. "Ghostwriter has a message."

The words spelled FIND OUT.

WE WILL, Tina wrote back. She looked at the others. "But how?"

Jamal snapped his fingers. "The main library is on Forty-second Street. We're on Forty-fourth."

"Let's go," Gaby said excitedly.

"Hold on," Jamal said. "Some of us should finish examining the stage. And I think we should interview the stagehands ourselves."

"I don't want to be stuck in a library when Alex is missing," Hector said.

"No, Hector," Jamal said. "The research could be the key to the whole mystery. If we find out *why* Alex was taken, we might discover where he is."

Hector nodded. "Maybe you're right. I guess I'll go to the library. We can bring the books back here."

"I'll come with you," Gaby said.

"Okay," Jamal said. He looked at his watch. "We'll meet back here in an hour. If we don't have a lead by then, we'll have to call the police."

"But they said no police," Gaby said.

"Gaby, if we don't have any leads, we have to trust the police," Tina told her gently. "It's the only way to get Alex back."

"I guess you're right," Gaby said in a small voice.

"Before we split up, let's ask Ghostwriter if there's anything new with Alex," Hector suggested.

"Why don't we ask him if he can read anything else near Alex now?" Jamal said.

Tina nodded and wrote: CAN YOU READ ANYTHING NEAR ALEX NOW?

After a moment, the reply came. CALL ME CRAZY. THE MAN FROM LOUISIANA. BEAUTIFUL DREAMER.

Hector frowned. "Those look familiar."

"They're all the names of plays," Gaby said. "I saw them as we were walking to the theater."

"They were on the marquees of other theaters," Tina said excitedly. "Do you know what that means?"

"No," Hector admitted.

"Alex must be right here on Forty-fourth Street!" Tina exclaimed. "How else could Ghostwriter read the theater signs?"

"But there are so many buildings on this street," Hector said, discouraged. "He could be anywhere."

CAN YOU READ ANYTHING ELSE? Tina wrote.

A moment later, the reply came: RE MI DO FE.

Lenni peered at it. "What is that—some kind of musical scale? It should be fa, not fe."

"Is the kidnapper a musician who can't spell?" Gaby wondered.

Everyone pondered the message, but nobody could figure it out.

"We'd better get moving," Jamal said finally. "We're not getting anywhere just standing here."

"Maybe Ghostwriter's message has something to do with the czarevitch," Gaby said.

"There's only one way to find out," Hector said. "Let's hit the library."

Jamal, Tina, and Lenni circled around the booth again. "I just don't see where Alex could have gone," Tina said in frustration. "I've crawled in and out of the booth and the secret compartment twelve times."

"There's a trapdoor on the stage, but it's on the other side," Jamal said. "The booth was right here, wasn't it?"

"Definitely," Tina said.

"Let's go talk to the stagehands," Lenni suggested.

They found the head of the stagehand crew backstage, filling the white garbage can with fruit peelings and coffee grounds for the next show. He told them that he was the only stagehand who had watched the trick. But he hadn't seen a thing.

"Are you sure you didn't see anything unusual at all?" Lenni urged.

The stagehand shook his head. "I was watching the trick from the wings stage left, so I didn't have the best view. But I would have seen the kid if he'd gone out the back."

Lenni sighed. "Thanks, anyway." She and Tina and Jamal headed to the front row of the theater, where they slumped in the first row of seats.

"What next, Jamal?" Tina asked. "You always know what to do."

He looked at them helplessly. "Not this time. We only have another twenty minutes before we have to call the police."

"But we might put Alex in danger!" Lenni said.

Jamal frowned worriedly. "I know," he said.

Alex slumped against the wall of the round room. It was beginning to feel like a prison. He was hungry and cold and a little scared. What was going on? Were his friends trying to find him? He just had to know. He formed the letters:

GW: ?

Soon, Ghostwriter used the letters on the peanut bag to send him a message. One by one, the words came.

WAIT

HOPE

WE ARE

WITH YOU

Alex looked at the glowing words. Ghostwriter didn't have many letters to work with. But he still managed to tell Alex that his friends were on the case. He still was able to show Alex how much he cared. Feeling better, Alex settled in to wait.

Gaby and Hector ran all the way to Forty-second Street and Fifth Avenue. They paused, panting, on the steps of the library. The massive building loomed above them. Columns lined the front and a pair of stone lions guarded the stairs.

"Wow," Hector said. "Are you sure regular people like us can go in there?"

"Libraries are for everybody," Gaby said.

"I know that," Hector said. "But this one looks like it's for everybody but us." He cast a lion a sidelong glance. "He knows I'm from Brooklyn."

"We're doing this for Alex, remember," Gaby said firmly. She grabbed Hector's hand and pulled him toward the entrance.

Inside, they went up stone stairs to a large room that

was filled with computers on one side and books on the other. A long desk ran down the middle. Busy librarians directed people with questions or took little slips of paper from them.

"First things first," Gaby said. She spied a large dictionary sitting on its own small table in one corner. "Let's look up czarevitch."

Quickly, they flipped through the book. Gaby read the listing out loud: " 'Czarevitch: the eldest son of a czar of Russia; prince.' "

"Prince!" Hector exclaimed. "Remember the note? 'Beware of false princes.' But I still don't get it."

"Let's look up the Russian Revolution," Gaby suggested. "Maybe it will make sense then."

At the desk, a friendly librarian explained how the system worked. "This is a research library," she told them. "You can't check out books—you have to read them here."

"Oh, no!" Gaby exclaimed.

"We have a very nice reading room," the librarian said with a smile.

"I guess we have no choice," Gaby said. "But we'll have to hurry," she told Hector.

"The card catalog is computerized," the librarian explained. "Just type in your book title, author, or subject. The computer will list all the books that we have. Then fill out a call slip for each book and bring it to me."

Gaby and Hector thanked her and went to the bank of computers. Gaby sat down at the computer and typed out *Russian Revolution*. Immediately, a list of titles began to appear on the screen.

"Where should we start?" Hector wondered. "We don't have time to go through all these books."

"Let's pick the ones that were published in the last couple of years," Gaby suggested.

Together they picked out five books. Then they filled out five call slips. Suddenly, the screen went blank and a message flashed at them.

GOOD WORK!

"Ghostwriter!" Gaby whispered. "Let's ask how Alex is."

She typed in: HOW IS ALEX?

The message came back. OK. BUT SCARED, I THINK.

Hector reached over to tap out a message. PLEASE TELL HIM WE'RE TRYING HARD.

Ghostwriter flashed back: I ALREADY DID. KEEP TRYING. IF ANYONE CAN FIND ALEX, THE TEAM CAN.

Hector and Gaby exchanged grins. Ghostwriter believed in them. That helped a lot.

Gaby typed out, WHY CAN'T ALEX GIVE US MORE INFORMATION?

A moment later, the letters appeared. I'M NOT SURE. MAYBE HE LOST HIS PEN OR HAS NO PAPER. SOMETIMES HIS LETTERS ARE HARD TO READ.

Hector tapped out: CAN ALEX TELL US HOW HE DISAPPEARED?

It seemed to take a long time before the next message appeared: MESSAGE FROM ALEX: TRAP

"Trap?" Hector asked. He looked at Gaby. "What does it mean? Is Alex caught in a trap? Are *we* heading for a trap?"

Gaby shook her head. "We don't have time to figure it out now. Let's hit the books. The team is counting on us."

They handed the call slips to the librarian, then waited impatiently for their number to light up on the board.

"This is worse than waiting for messages from Alex," Gaby said, hopping from one foot to the other.

Hector bit his lip. "Time is running out. We only have twenty minutes more."

Finally, their number lit up. The librarian handed them a stack of thick books. They rushed to an empty table. Quickly, they began to flip through the pages.

" 'The last czar of Russia was called Nicholas the Second,' " Gaby read aloud. " 'His family name was Romanov. He and his wife and children were killed in 1918 by the Bolsheviks.' " Gaby looked up. "He had four daughters and a son. That's so sad."

"The son's name was Alexis," Hector said. "He was the czarevitch—the prince and heir."

"The Bolsheviks were also called the Red Army," Gaby said, scanning her book.

She turned to a blank page in her notebook and wrote: *The czar and his family were killed in 1918. Their last name was Romanov. The name of the czarevitch (prince) was Alexis. They were killed by the Red Army (the Bolsheviks).* Then she turned back to her book.

"Check this out," she said. "It says here that there are still descendants of the Romanov family. Then there are other people who also say they're in the line of succession, including the Kropotkins and the Ranevskys."

"What's a line of succession?" Hector asked.

"That means that there are people living today who say that they're related to the Russian royal family," Gaby explained, her finger on her book. "That means they could be in line to inherit the throne of Russia. Even though there is no throne in Russia now. They're still working out their new government."

Hector shook his head in disbelief. "I *still* don't get what this has to do with Alex."

"The note said *give up your claims,* remember?" Gaby reminded him excitedly. "What if somebody thinks that Alex is claiming to be the prince?"

"That's crazy," Hector exclaimed. "How could anyone make such a big mistake?"

"I know," Gaby admitted, tapping the page of the book. "I mean, the Fernandez line to the throne does sound weird.

There sure aren't many Russian czars running around in El Salvador!"

Suddenly, all the numbers on the board over their heads began to light up crazily.

"Ghostwriter must be trying to signal us," Hector guessed.

They handed their books back to the desk. Then they hurried to the computer. Hector typed out: GHOSTWRITER, DO YOU HAVE A MESSAGE FOR US?

The screen glowed. MESSAGE FROM ALEX CONTINUED: DOOR

"Door," Hector repeated. "What does that mean? That Alex went through a door?"

"Remember, the message is *continued*," Gaby said. "I think I know what Alex means. Let's go!"

Attention, Reader 🔊
Can you figure out Alex's Message?
—Ghostwriter

"Let's go over the clues one more time," Jamal suggested.

Lenni groaned and shifted in her seat. "My eyes will fall out if I read the casebook again. There's nothing new in it, anyway."

"Lenni's right, Jamal," Tina said gloomily.

☆ **65** ☆

Jamal stared down at the casebook. "Hey, you didn't enter what the stagehand said under *Evidence*."

Lenni blew out an exasperated breath. "That's because 'I didn't see the kid' isn't exactly evidence."

"Actually, he said he didn't have the best *view*, but he *would* have seen the kid if he left from the rear," Tina corrected.

"Whatever," Lenni said. "He was in the wings stage left." She looked up at the stage. "I wonder why he had a bad view? The booth was stage left."

"No, it wasn't," Tina said. "It was on the right."

"From *our* perspective, yeah," Lenni said. "But *stage left* and *stage right* are from the performer's perspective."

"Huh?" Tina asked.

"They're both theater terms," Lenni explained. "If you're standing on the stage looking *out* at the audience, stage left is on your left. But from the audience, it's the right side of the stage."

"Lenni, could you speak English, please?" Jamal asked.

Lenni grinned and turned to a blank page in her notebook. Quickly, she sketched a view of the stage. Then she drew a picture of the booth.

"You see?" Lenni said. "We saw the booth on the *right* side of the stage. But for someone standing center stage looking out at us, it was on the *left*. Stage left. It's the opposite. Get it?"

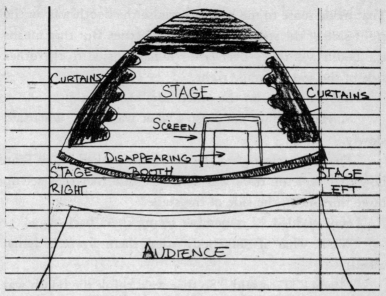

"I guess so," Tina said. "It's kind of confusing, though."

Jamal stared at the sketch. Suddenly, he jumped up and ran toward the wings. "You're a genius, Lenni!"

"I know," Lenni said, sitting up. "But what did I say this time?"

"I'll be right back!" Jamal called, disappearing into the wings.

Lenni and Tina exchanged puzzled glances, then shrugged. They didn't have long to wait. In a little while, Jamal was back.

"I had to double-check something with Finn," Jamal said excitedly. "Earlier, he said the booth was *stage right.*

That made sense to me before, because the booth was on the right side of the stage from our perspective. But that means the booth was really over *here*." Jamal crossed to the other side of the stage—stage right.

"But we saw it on the other side," Lenni said.

"Maybe what we *saw* wasn't what was *there*," Tina said slowly.

"That's exactly right," Jamal said. "I asked Riley Finn how that skeleton trick was done. He said that they set up huge mirrors on the side of the stage."

Lenni nodded. "I remember seeing them backstage."

"Well, what if somebody used them *again*?" Jamal asked.

"I know!" Tina said. "So that we'd think the booth was on the *right* side instead of the left!"

Jamal waved his hands. "The important thing is that *the booth wasn't where we thought it was.* It was right here and not over there."

"So what does that mean?" Lenni asked.

"It means now we know how Alex disappeared," Jamal said triumphantly. He hit the stage with a sneakered foot. "The booth was over a—"

"Trapdoor!" Gaby yelled as she ran down the aisle of the theater.

Everyone ran up on stage and stared down at the trapdoor. Jamal reached down and pushed a metal handle set into the stage. The door swung down and they saw blackness below.

Jamal peered into the hole. "There's a chute."

Hector looked uneasy. "What if the kidnappers are down there?"

"Then Alex is too," Gaby said. She sat down and swung her legs into the hole. "I'm going."

"Gaby, maybe we should—" Jamal started, but Gaby pushed off and zoomed down the chute.

Tina dropped to her knees and looked into the hole. "Gaby? Gaby? Are you okay?"

Gaby's voice was shaky. "I'm fine. But it's awfully dark down here."

"I'll be right down," Jamal said. He swung his legs over the side and disappeared. "Come on down!" he called a few seconds later. "I'm going to look for a light switch."

One by one, the team slid down the chute. They landed softly on a dusty mattress. Tina was the last one down, and she rolled a little farther than the others. Her hand hit a familiar object.

"It's Alex's pen!" she cried, holding it up in the gloom.

"He was here!" Gaby said.

Jamal found a light switch in the far corner. He turned it on, but there wasn't much to see. Just brick walls, a stone floor, and wooden shelves lining one wall. Some old theatrical lights were piled in a corner. There was a staircase in one corner of the room near a door marked EXIT.

Hector pushed the door open. Fresh air blew in. The door led to an alley that sloped upward toward the street.

"They could have taken him out this way pretty easily," Tina said, discouraged. "All they had to do was back a car into the alley."

Lenni saw something red glinting up at her. She bent down and picked it up. "Look, a matchbook," she said. "Maybe it's a clue. It's from a restaurant called the Black Sea Café in Brighton Beach. In Brooklyn."

"Anyone could have dropped that," Jamal said.

"Well, anyway, we know that Alex isn't there," Tina said. "We know he's on Forty-fourth Street."

"I'm going to enter it in the casebook anyway," Lenni said.

Suddenly Hector exclaimed, "Hey, look! There's an elevator here. Alex could have been brought this way."

"But why would they bring him back upstairs?" Jamal asked. "They'd risk being seen."

Tina pushed the Up button. "We should check it out, just in case."

The inside of the elevator was completely empty. "Another dead end," Lenni said, discouraged.

"Look!" Gaby cried. "Otis!"

Lenni looked around wildly. "Where is he?"

"There," Gaby said, pointing to the elevator floor. The name of the manufacturer was in raised letters on the metal runner near the door. OTIS.

Tina pointed to the floor buttons: 12345. "It's our clue! Ghostwriter must have read the name Otis and these numbers when Alex was in the elevator. Let's go!"

They all crowded onto the small elevator and stared at the floor buttons. Lenni flipped the casebook open. "Let's see if Alex can tell us which button to push." She wrote: GHOSTWRITER, PLEASE ASK ALEX IF HE CAN TELL IF HE'S HIGH UP.

They waited impatiently. Finally, Ghostwriter used OTIS and the name of the last elevator inspector, D. P. Ruben, to spell OUT.

"We want to know if he's *up*, not *out*, whatever that means," Gaby said impatiently.

"Wait," Lenni said. "Alex takes a while to give us a complete message."

In another few seconds, the next word glowed: SIDE.

"The roof," Jamal said. He pressed the button for the fifth floor.

The elevator cranked slowly up the shaft to a landing at the top of some narrow stairs. There was a door to the right. Gaby pushed it open and they spilled out onto the roof. Everyone scanned the open space frantically.

"Alex!" Gaby cried in frustration.

Lenni looked around. "Look how close the buildings are together. It would be pretty easy to jump over and take him to another building."

"Especially if you were with the circus," Hector said gloomily. "Remember the knife?"

"That's right," Gaby said, her face downcast.

Tina frowned. "Maybe we should call the police now. It's getting late."

Hector beat his fist against the brick wall. "We can't give up! Not yet!"

"But Hector, the kidnappers could have gone anywhere from here," Lenni pointed out.

Suddenly, Gaby's mouth dropped open. She flung her arm out and pointed. "Look!"

Everyone looked. All they could see was an almost empty billboard. But then they saw the words:

ER

MI

D O   FE

"Ghostwriter's clue!" Tina said.

"It's not a musical scale!" Lenni exclaimed. "It's a billboard!"

"We saw it before," Jamal said. "The man was ripping it down, remember? 'After theater, please make mine Pyrlando Coffee.'"

"Alex must be very near," Gaby said excitedly.

Tina flipped open the casebook. "Let's look at the clues again. We got OTIS 12345 and RE MI DO FE. But what about the letter *O*?"

"When did Alex send us that message?" Jamal asked.

Tina checked the casebook. "We asked him to describe where he was. He sent back the letter *O*." She looked up. "I'm stumped."

Suddenly, the sun slipped below the billboard, blinding her. Tina shielded her eyes. The sun was so bright and round. . . .

"Wait a second!" Tina exclaimed. "Maybe it wasn't the letter *O* that Alex meant. We asked him to *describe* where he

☆ 75 ☆

was. Maybe he meant to tell us that he was in someplace *round*."

"Someplace round?" Gaby asked. "Like that revolving hotel restaurant over on Times Square? I'll kill Alex if he's sitting there eating a cheeseburger while we're sweating our brains out."

Suddenly, Jamal laughed. "He's not in a restaurant," he said. He pointed to a round wooden water tower near the edge of the roof. It sat on stilts. It was small but sturdy, and there would be plenty of room for Alex.

"Alex!" Gaby shouted. Everyone started to run. When they got to the tower, they beat on it with their fists. They heard an answering thump.

"Alex!" Hector cried.

There was a small metal ladder curving up the side of the tower. Gaby was the first to jump on it and scramble to the top. She peeked over the top and saw her brother's dark eyes twinkling up at her.

"It's about time," Alex said. "I'm starving!"

CHAPTER

9

Gaby grinned. "Some guys will do *anything* for attention."

"Get me out of here!" Alex said.

Jamal found a portable ladder underneath the tower. Gaby scrambled down, and Jamal scrambled up.

He looked down at Alex. "What's up, my man?"

"Oh, not much," Alex said. "Just hanging."

Jamal laughed. He hooked the portable ladder onto the side of the tower and let it fall down the other side. In seconds, Alex climbed out.

Gaby threw her arms around him, and then Hector hugged him shyly. Tina just stood there, her dark eyes shining.

Lenni shook Alex playfully. "You gave us quite a scare, Fernandez."

"What happened to you?" Gaby demanded.

"Who took you?" Tina asked.

"Did they say anything?" Hector asked.

Alex held up his hands. "Whoa, slow down. I don't know who took me. Or why. How did you guys find me?"

"Hold on, everybody," Jamal interrupted. He looked around anxiously. "We can compare notes later. The kidnappers could come back any minute."

"Wait!" Lenni cried. She scribbled in her notebook as fast as she could. GW: WE FOUND ALEX!

A second later, Ghostwriter's glow dipped into the notebook, searching for letters. Soon a message appeared and hung shimmering in the air: GOOD WORK! NOW HURRY TO SAFETY.

The team didn't need any more urging. They ran across the rooftop to the stairs and started down. On the third landing, Jamal held up his hand.

"I hear talking," he whispered. "Wait here, and I'll check it out."

"I'll come with you," Tina whispered.

The two tiptoed farther down the stairs. Jamal paused. "We must be close to the dressing rooms," he whispered.

Tina nodded. Now they could hear the voices more clearly. It was Galina and Riley Finn.

"Harry is still on the phone with our press agent," Riley

Finn complained. "He's scared those kids will call the police."

"Maybe they should," Galina said. "Those poor kids. You guys sure haven't been much help."

"Harry won't let me call the police," Finn said. "He's not a U.S. citizen. He's afraid he'll get deported back to Russia."

Tina's wide eyes met Jamal's. Harry Sawchuck was Russian!

"Listen," Finn said, "I haven't eaten all day. I'm going to run out for a sandwich. Want to come? Or will Leo get jealous?"

Galina sounded irritated. "Leo is in Chicago, and I'm not hungry."

"Aw, come on," Finn said. "You're not Mrs. Kropotkin yet."

"Maybe *you* should disappear," Galina said.

Jamal touched Tina's arm and nodded toward the stairs. With Riley Finn still teasing Galina, they had time to get away. Tina signaled the team.

Everyone tiptoed nervously down the stairs and out the exit. Quickly, they ran down the alley and all the way down Forty-fourth Street. They didn't stop until they reached the subway.

"I'm so tired," Gaby moaned. "Foiling a kidnapping is hard work."

"Sorry to put you to all that trouble," Alex teased her. "Now, would you guys mind telling me *why* I was kidnapped? It can't be for the ransom."

"Wait. Shouldn't we tell Sawchuck and Finn that we found Alex?" Lenni asked. "We don't know for sure if one of them kidnapped him."

"Sawchuck and Finn?" Alex asked, surprised.

"I'll call them," Jamal said. "It can't do any harm now."

While Jamal went to the phone, Tina flipped open the casebook. She went through the events of the day slowly, pointing the various clues out to Alex. "There's one more clue," she told the others. "Harry Sawchuck is Russian. We heard Riley Finn say it."

"That makes him our prime suspect," Jamal said as he returned. "He sounded relieved on the phone, but he could have been faking. He looked awfully strange when he read the kidnap note. I bet he recognized the word *czarevitch*."

"He could have saved us a trip to the library," Gaby said.

"Czarevitch," Alex murmured. "Wait a second. That's the word the kidnapper said to me as he left! What do I have to do with some Russian prince?"

"We haven't figured that out yet," Hector admitted. "The last czarevitch died in 1918. His name was Alexis—"

"Hold on!" Alex said to Jamal excitedly. "Remember the kid who was sitting next to me?"

Jamal nodded. "Sure. The snob who wouldn't give up the seat."

"His name was *Alexis,*" Alex said.

"Talk about coincidences," Jamal said. "Maybe he's Russian too."

The team was silent as the information sank in. Then everybody began to talk at once.

"Wait," Tina said. "I bet that—"

"Maybe the kidnappers—" Lenni said.

"Thought Alex was Alexis!" everyone said at once.

"They kidnapped the wrong kid!" Jamal said. "They probably didn't know what Alex looked like."

"You mean they didn't know what *Alexis* looked like," Gaby corrected.

"Maybe they knew *around* where Alexis would be sitting and a general description," Tina suggested.

Lenni jumped up. "Come on, here's the train."

They piled onto the train and found seats together.

"You know what this means," Tina said over the roar of the train. "We can eliminate some suspects. Like Riley Finn. His only motive would be to get Sawchuck back by sabotaging the show."

Lenni yawned. "I'm too tired to figure anything out. Let's go over everything tomorrow."

"Wait. We're forgetting something important," Jamal said. "The kidnappers got the wrong Alex. Sooner or later they'll probably figure it out."

Gaby gasped. "Alexis! He's still in danger!"

"We have to warn him," Tina said.

"But how?" Lenni asked. "We don't even know his last name."

"I think it's time we called Lieutenant McQuade," Jamal said.

Everyone nodded. "I'll do it when I get home," Jamal added. "Then, tomorrow morning, we can meet and go over the case. We might be able to give Lieutenant McQuade some clues."

"Come to my house," Lenni said. "Dad has an early rehearsal tomorrow. He'll buy plenty of bagels and stuff before he goes."

"Bagels? We're there," Jamal said.

Jamal phoned the station house as soon as he got home. But Lieutenant McQuade wasn't there. "Try tomorrow," the sergeant said.

Jamal drummed his fingers anxiously. "Okay. But can I talk to someone else tonight?"

The desk sergeant put Jamal on hold. A moment later, a female voice barked "Detective Samson" into the receiver.

Jamal told her all he knew. She didn't interrupt, just

kept saying "uh-huh" and "I see." Finally, he stopped. There was a long pause.

"Aren't you a little old to be making crank calls to the police?" Detective Samson said.

"It's not a crank call," Jamal protested.

"Someone kidnapped your friend Fernandez, thinking he was the prince of Russia," Detective Samson repeated wearily. "The last of the Romanovs, right? Disappearing acts, czars, circus knives, water towers—yeah, *right*. Listen, I have work to do, kid. Don't call again."

Jamal heard a click and then the harsh buzz of a dial tone.

CHAPTER

☆ **10** ☆

Early Sunday morning, the team met at Lenni's loft. Jamal shut the door behind him in frustration.

"Lieutenant McQuade is at the dentist having emergency root canal this morning," he said. "I had to talk to Detective Samson again. Last night she didn't believe me. Today she told me she'd write out a warrant for my arrest if I called again."

"Oh, no," Lenni said. "What are we going to do?"

"We're going to find Alexis by ourselves," Jamal said determinedly.

Everyone looked nervous for a minute. Then Tina put down her bagel. "Well, we'd better get started, then."

Lenni flipped open the casebook. "Let's go over the reasons why Sawchuck is a suspect," she said. "Number one, he's Russian and didn't tell us when he read that note. That's suspicious."

"And he didn't tell us that the booth had been moved," Tina pointed out.

"Maybe he didn't know," Hector said. "He said he didn't watch the trick."

"But how do we know he was telling the truth?" Gaby asked.

"Hold on," Tina said. "I just remembered something. Sawchuck asked Galina if the knife was a circus knife. Maybe that means she was in the circus with him."

"And we're pretty sure Sawchuck was in a Russian circus," Jamal said. "We saw the poster for a Russian circus in his dressing room."

Lenni chewed on her pen. "So Galina could be Russian too. We can't rule her out as a suspect."

"Let's not forget that we need to warn Alexis," Tina said. "Alex, what do you remember about him?"

Alex thought a moment. "He and the bald guy were heading for the D train when they left."

Lenni wrote down, *Could live near a stop on the D line.*

"He likes peanuts," Alex said with a grin. "Only his father or whoever that was wouldn't let him eat any." Alex frowned in concentration. "He said to wait and eat in Little Something . . . "

"Little Italy?" Gaby guessed.

"No," Alex said. "Something with *s*'s in it. Little Odessa!"

"Let's get out the subway map," Hector suggested. "Maybe Little Odessa is one of the stops on the D train."

Lenni jumped up and got the subway map. She handed it to Alex.

Alex groaned as he pored over the map. "The D train goes just about everywhere—Manhattan, Brooklyn, and the Bronx."

Suddenly, letters began to appear in the casebook. "It's Ghostwriter!" Tina exclaimed.

BEST PIROGIES IN BROOKLYN. BLACK SEA CAFE.

"My matchbook!" Lenni exclaimed. She dug into the pocket of her overalls. "I forgot to enter it in the casebook yesterday."

"What's a pirogi?" Hector asked.

Just then, Max walked in from the kitchen area. "Pirogies are delicious," he said. "They're pastries, stuffed with meat or vegetables. Kind of like a turnover, Russian style."

The team exchanged glances. Russian! Things were starting to add up.

"Gotta go, gang," Max said. He leaned over and kissed the top of Lenni's head.

The door closed behind Max. Lenni showed the team the matchbook. "Look." She turned the matchbook over and read aloud, " 'Black Sea Café, Brighton Beach, Brooklyn.' "

Jamal looked at the subway map. "Hey, Brighton Beach is a stop on the D train."

"Now we're getting someplace," Gaby said in a satisfied tone. She paused. "Uh, where are we getting, exactly?"

"Maybe it would help if we knew where 'big' Odessa was," Tina said. "There should be one, right? Kind of like Little Italy and 'big' Italy."

Lenni ran to get the atlas. She handed it to Tina. "Here you go. I'm going to look up Brighton Beach in the New York guidebook."

After a moment, Tina looked up from the atlas. "Guys, you aren't going to believe this. Odessa is a port on the *Black Sea*. In the former Soviet Union."

Lenni squealed and looked up from the guidebook. "Listen up. 'Brighton Beach has a fast-growing population of Russian and Ukrainian immigrants. Residents sometimes refer to the area as *Little Odessa*.'"

"Let's rock," Jamal said.

Twenty minutes later, the team stood in front of the Black Sea Café. A sign read that the café didn't open for another half hour. Alex knocked on the door anyway. There was no answer.

They turned around and looked at the boardwalk running along the ocean. People were strolling along or sitting at outside cafés. Brighton Beach would be fun to explore.

Tina looked carefully at the signs on the shops and restaurants. "The letters look like the ones I saw in the old photograph in Harry's dressing room," she told the team.

"I looked up Russia in the encyclopedia last night," Jamal said. "They have a different alphabet. It's called Cyrillic."

A man wearing an old jacket and a tweed hat walked up. He passed them and started to open the restaurant door with a key. A sudden gust of wind blew his hat away, and Alex picked it up. When he went to return it, he saw that the man was bald. It was the man who'd been with Alexis!

"Excuse me," Alex said. "Didn't we meet at the theater yesterday?"

The bald man frowned. Then he brightened. "Oh, yes—the boy with the peanuts."

"I have a very important message for Alexis," Alex said. "I know it seems strange. But please, I have to talk to him."

The man gave a warm smile. "He's my nephew," he said as he turned to unlock the door. "He'll be along for breakfast any minute. Would you and your friends like to wait inside?"

"Thank you," Alex said, following him.

"My name is Vladimir Petrov," the man said.

"I'm Alex Fernandez," Alex said. He introduced the rest of the team.

As Vladimir ushered them into the restaurant, Alexis appeared. He glanced at them, then turned to his uncle. "What's going on?"

"These children have come to see you, Alexis," Vladimir said.

Alexis sighed. "So? I'm hungry."

Alex wondered why he was bothering to warn such a nasty kid. "We think you're in danger."

"Why would I be in danger?" Alexis scoffed.

Vladimir froze, a stack of menus in his hands. "Yes, why would a boy like Alexis be in danger?"

"Because he might be the czarevitch," Alex said calmly.

The menus slid out of Vladimir's hands and dropped to the floor with a clatter. "How do you know?" he asked hoarsely. "No one besides our family knows that Alexis is the descendant of the third cousin once removed of the second cousin of Nicolas II."

"The what of the who of the which?" Gaby murmured.

"*Somebody* knows," Alex insisted.

"Yesterday, Alex was kidnapped," Jamal said. "We think he was mistaken for Alexis."

Alexis waved his hands, smiling. "You Americans! So excitable. Too much TV."

"We're serious. These people could be dangerous," Lenni said.

Vladimir sat down, wiping his forehead with a napkin. "This is impossible," he murmured.

"Vladimir!" The voice was strong and accented and came from the hallway. "Get in here!"

"It's Boris," Vladimir explained. "My boss. I'd better get to work. He's a good man. His daughter gave us the two free tickets to the magic show. She and Boris worked in the circus with Harry Sawchuck, and he gave her a job."

"Is Boris's daughter's name Galina?" Gaby asked excitedly.

Vladimir nodded.

"And they're Russian?" Gaby asked.

Vladimir nodded. "Of course."

Jamal hit his head. "I should have remembered before. I heard Riley Finn say that Galina is engaged to someone named Kropotkin. That sounds like a Russian name."

"Kropotkin?" Gaby looked at Hector. "Wasn't that the name of one of the families who claim to be in line to inherit the throne?"

"Kropotkin is a popular Russian name," Vladimir said uneasily. "I'm sure that Galina has nothing to do with a kidnapping scheme. She is a very sweet girl." Shaking his head, he went out.

The team wasn't so sure. Galina had just shot to the top of their list of suspects.

"Galina could have found out through her father that Alexis claims to be the czarevitch," Tina said in a low voice.

"Not *claims*," Alexis said haughtily. *"Is."*

"And she's engaged to someone who could be Alexis's rival for the Russian throne," Hector said. "That's motive."

"And she had plenty of opportunity to kidnap Alex," Lenni said. "She was behind the screen and could have opened the trapdoor."

"Hey," Jamal said. "Remember when Riley Finn was going to show us the booth and Galina was outside in the hall?"

"She could have been eavesdropping," Tina said.

"Not only that," Jamal said. "She could have let the rabbits out of the cages as a diversion. She didn't *want* Finn to show us the booth."

"Because he would have told us that it had been moved!" Gaby said.

Suddenly, the letters on the Black Sea Café menu began to glow. Ghostwriter! The letters re-formed into one word: BEWARE!

Alex jumped up. "We're in danger."

"You keep *saying* that," Alexis said. "But I must assure you, no one would dare to touch my imperial highness."

"Wanna bet?" Gaby growled. She was getting tired of Alexis the snob.

Alex decided to investigate. "I'll be right back," he told the others. He tiptoed around the corner.

Suddenly, a hood was thrown over his head from behind. His arms were twisted behind his back and his wrists were tied.

"Help!" he cried, but a hand was clapped over his mouth. Alex gave a muffled groan. Not again!

Gaby twisted around. "Did you hear that?"

"It sounded like Alex," Tina said.

Suddenly, letters began to fly off the menu. They hung in the air, glowing insistently.

HELP HIM!

Gaby jumped up. "Alex! Hurry!"

Everyone dashed out of the restaurant toward the hallway.

"What's going on?" Alexis called. He got up and followed.

The team ran down the hallway and burst into the kitchen. Vladimir was stacking plates.

"Have you seen Alex?" Gaby panted.

"No. Why—"

But the team didn't have time to answer. They dashed out of the kitchen. There was another door down the corridor. Jamal turned the knob and burst in. The rest of the team tumbled in after him.

Galina stood in the middle of the room. She was dressed in her outfit from the show, and was knotting together some colorful silk scarves. She looked at them, surprised.

"How nice to see you again. But the restaurant is the other way," she said politely.

"Where is he?" Jamal demanded.

Galina frowned. "Who?"

"Alex."

"Your friend? I thought that you found him yesterday." Galina knotted another scarf. She unfurled a line of silk scarves: pink, yellow, green, and aquamarine. Then she tugged on one end. All the scarves separated and floated to the carpet. "Please, I'm rehearsing," Galina said.

Gaby pushed forward. "Where is he?"

"If you've lost your friend again, I cannot help you," Galina said more sternly. "Please. You can see that I am alone."

The team looked around. The room was bare except for a cabinet. There was no door except the one they came through.

"The cabinet!" Gaby said accusingly.

"What about it?" Galina asked. "It's a wedding present for my father's niece in Russia."

"Can we see what's inside?" Jamal asked.

Galina shrugged. She went over and opened the door. The cabinet was empty. "So you see, your friend isn't here."

Suddenly, a burly man pushed past them into the room. "What is it, little one?" he asked Galina.

"They've lost their friend," she said. "It has nothing to do with us, Papa."

Papa! The man must be Boris.

"We think it does," Jamal said.

"And why is that?" Galina asked.

"Because yesterday you set up mirrors so that the audience would think the booth was on the other side of the stage. You pushed Alex down the trapdoor. And I would guess that you"—Jamal pointed to Boris—"carried Alex to the roof."

"This is ridiculous," Galina said.

"You two worked in the circus together," Jamal said. "Didn't you?"

"So?" Boris said.

"So it would be easy for you to carry Alex all that way. Easy to balance on a little metal ladder," Lenni said shrewdly.

"Don't listen to them, Papa," Galina said.

Vladimir appeared in the doorway. "What's going on? Boris, people outside are knocking."

"I'll go to them." Suddenly, Boris stopped in his tracks. "What is he doing here?" he asked, pointing to Alexis.

Vladimir put his arm on Alexis's shoulder. He looked confused. "This is my nephew Alexis. You've met him."

Boris turned to Galina. "*That* is Alexis!" he cried.

Galina went pale. "That one?"

"You did it again, you two," Jamal said. "You kidnapped the wrong kid!"

Galina shook back her blond hair. "I don't know what you mean," she said nervously. "Why don't we discuss it in the restaurant?"

"Stop!" Gaby cried. Everyone turned toward her.

"I learned something yesterday," Gaby said, facing them. "When it comes to magic, things are never what they seem."

She crossed over to the cabinet and thrust her hand inside. But suddenly, everyone saw two hands instead of one.

"A mirror!" Tina breathed.

It was true. There was a mirror in the cabinet. Set at an angle, it reflected the wooden sides so that the cabinet appeared empty. Gaby felt along the seams of the mirror and found a tiny lever. She pressed it, and the mirror swung down. Alex tumbled out, a hood over his head and his hands tied behind his back.

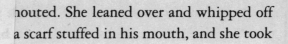

houted. She leaned over and whipped off a scarf stuffed in his mouth, and she took

ral deep breaths. "Thanks," he said to w sisters could come in so handy."

"That is not the right boy!" Boris thundered to Galina. He pointed to Alexis. *"That* is the boy! That is the pretender to the throne!"

"I thought—you said—" Galina stammered.

"This is no time to argue," Boris said. He and Galina pushed past the team.

Now everyone could hear the knocking on the front door get louder. The team hurried down the hall after Boris and Galina. They reached the restaurant just as Lieutenant McQuade burst in.

"It's them!" Alex shouted, pointing at Galina and Boris. "They tried to kidnap me—twice!"

Boris made a dash for the door, but he was stopped by two police officers. Lieutenant McQuade slapped handcuffs on Galina.

Everything was in an uproar for the next few minutes. While Lieutenant McQuade read Galina and Boris their rights, they kept interrupting to argue with each other. Then, when Lieutenant McQuade was finished, they turned on Vladimir and Alexis.

"There is only one true czarevitch!" Boris bellow[ed]

"That's right!" Vladimir said. "And he's standing r[ight] here!"

"His name is Leonid Kropotkin and he is in Chicago!" Galina sputtered. "One day, when Russia realizes her true destiny, Leo will be czar. And I will be czarina!"

"You're all bonkers," Lieutenant McQuade said.

"Tell me something," Vladimir said. "How did you know about Alexis? We told no one."

"Papa overheard you talking at breakfast one day," Galina said. "To think that someone would challenge Leo's claim!"

"Leo Kropotkin—phooey!" Alexis said. "He is only the descendant of the fourth cousin *twice* removed of the czar's great-aunt. Big deal!"

"I'm not getting any of this stuff," Gaby whispered to Tina.

"It's all relative," Tina said with a giggle.

Galina turned to Alexis furiously. "Watch your mouth, pip-squeak. I almost got you once. We were going to ship you to Siberia. You would never have been heard from again!"

"Now *there's* a thought," Jamal muttered.

"Be quiet, Galina!" Boris warned. "This is all your fault. You picked the wrong boy."

the third row! He was sitting next to

w that one"—Galina pointed to Gaby—

tell him the tickets were free!"

itting you kidnapped Alex?" Lieutenant

"I would do it again," Galina yelled. "The future of Mother Russia is at stake!"

"You mean Mother Russia who is twice removed from a fourth cousin on a great-aunt's side?" Vladimir sneered.

"My Leosha is the future imperial czar!" Galina announced regally.

"Never!" Vladimir bellowed.

"I need some aspirin," Lieutenant McQuade said. He rubbed his swollen jaw.

"Boy, were we glad to see you," Jamal said. "I never thought Detective Samson would give you that message."

"She didn't," Lieutenant McQuade said. "She told me about this 'crank call' as a joke. She wanted to get my mind off my sore tooth. It worked." He winced. "For a while."

"You saved my life," Alexis said to the team. "I will never forget this. When I am czar, I will reward you."

"I wouldn't hold my breath," Lieutenant McQuade told the team. He winked. "How did you all get mixed up with these crazy characters, anyway?"

"Magic," Jamal said, and they laughed.

Just as the police led Galina a~~~
chuck and Riley Finn showed up.

"Galina!" Sawchuck called. "What's going~
the police taking you away?"

"I am the future czarina!" Galina shouted.

"Watch your head, your highness," the officer said sar-
castically as he helped her into the car.

"What's happening here?" Riley Finn asked the team.
"We were supposed to have a meeting with Galina. What
is she doing?"

"Probably fifteen years to life," Lieutenant McQuade
said.

"We must celebrate!" Vladimir cried, disappearing into
the kitchen. "My borscht for everyone!"

"I'll see you later," Lieutenant McQuade told the team.
"Thanks for the help." He gave Jamal a sharp look. "Al-
though I still don't know how you do it. Oh, my tooth!"
He winced again and headed for the squad car.

Riley Finn frowned. "Will somebody *please* tell us what's
going on?"

"Boy, do we have a story for you," Gaby said.

Alex spooned up the last of his borscht, a delicious beet
soup. "So that's about it," he said. "Gaby found me in the
cabinet, and then the police came."

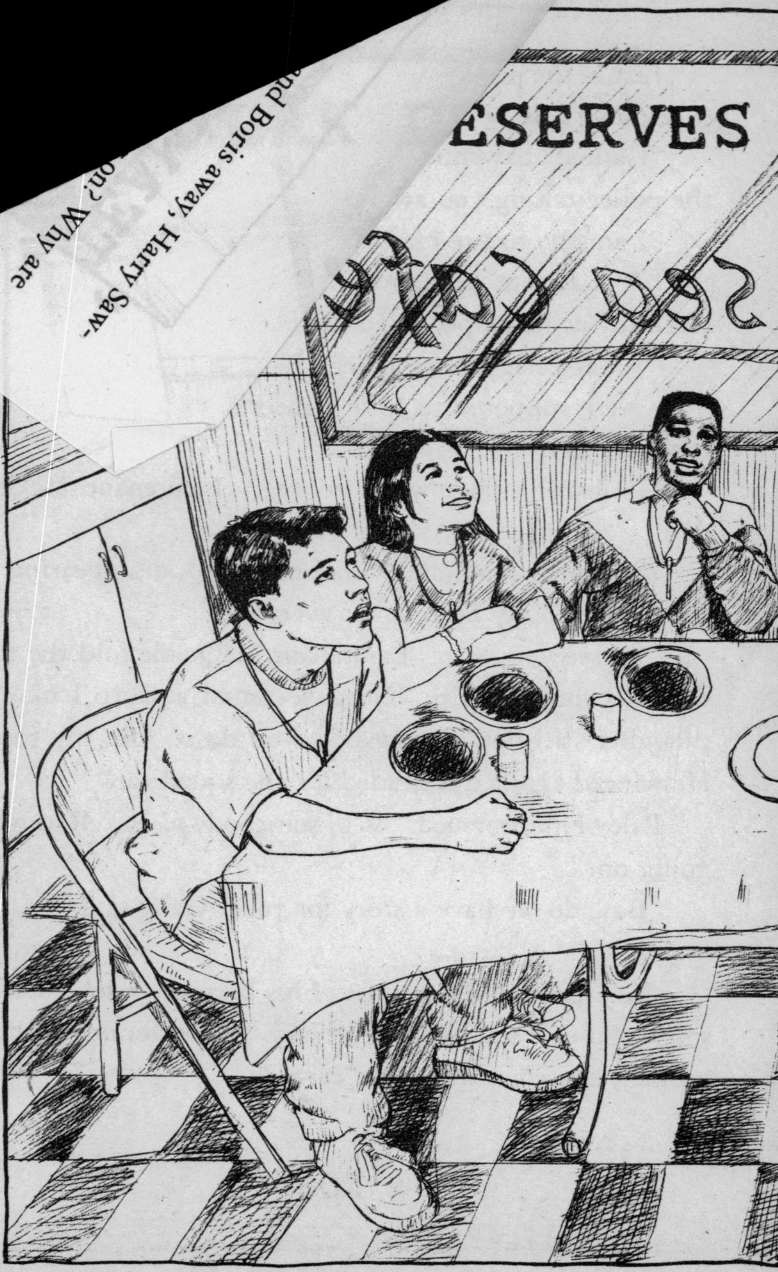
ESERVES

Harry Sawchuck frowned. "*I* was your main suspect?"

Tina laughed. "We're sorry. But you *did* seem suspicious."

"I was just afraid this weirdsmobile was playing a practical joke on me," Sawchuck said, pointing to Finn. "I thought all that Russian hocus-pocus was directed at me."

"Why would I play a joke on you?" Finn scoffed. "I have better things to do with my time."

"Like what?" Sawchuck asked. "Practice your magic? I should only *hope* so."

"I don't need to practice," Finn said. "Unlike *some* of us."

Alex rolled his eyes. "There they go again," he murmured as Finn and Sawchuck continued to argue.

"I guess being a team isn't so easy sometimes," Gaby said. "Remember how we were all irritable yesterday morning?"

"Ghostwriter keeps us on track," Tina said.

"Well, team, here we are in Little Odessa," Alex said. "What next?"

Suddenly, the framed restaurant review on the wall began to glow.

"I think Ghostwriter has a suggestion," Lenni said.

The letters floated into the air and hung there. They danced a bit, as if celebrating Alex's return.

TEAMWORK DESERVES REWARD. TRY PIROGIES.

From the Hit TV Show

GHOST writer

Created by CTW

BECOME AN OFFICIAL
GHOSTWRITER READERS CLUB MEMBER!

You'll receive the following GHOSTWRITER Readers Club Materials:
Official Membership Card • The Scoop on GHOSTWRITER •
GHOSTWRITER Magazine

All members registered by December 31st will have a chance to win
a FREE COMPUTER and other exciting prizes!

O F F I C I A L   E N T R Y   F O R M

Mail your completed entry to: Bantam Doubleday Dell BFYR,
GW Club, 1540 Broadway, New York, NY 10036

Name

Address

City   **State**   **Zip**

Age   **Phone**

Club Sweepstakes Official Rules
1. No purchase necessary. Enter by completing and returning the Entry Coupon. All entries must be received by Bantam Doubleday Dell no later than December 31, 1993. No mechanically reproduced entries allowed. By entering the sweepstakes, each entrant agrees to be bound by these rules and the decision of the judges which shall be final and binding. Limit: one entry per person.
2. The prizes are as follows: Grand Prize: One computer with monitor (approximate retail value of Grand Prize $3,000), First Prizes: Ten GHOSTWRITER libraries (approximate retail value of each First Prize: $25), Second Prizes: Five GHOSTWRITER backpacks (approximate retail value of each Second Prize: $25), and Third Prizes: Ten GHOSTWRITER T-Shirts (approximate retail value of each Third Prize: $10). Winners will be chosen in a random drawing on or about January 10, 1994, from among all completed Entry Coupons received and will be notified by mail. Odds of winning depend on the number of entries received. No substitution or transfer of the prize is allowed. All entries become property of BDD and will not be returned. Taxes, if any, are the sole responsibility of the winner. BDD reserves the right to substitute a prize of equal or greater value if any prize becomes unavailable.
3. This sweepstakes is open only to the residents of the U.S. and Canada, excluding the Province of Quebec, who are between the ages of 6 and 14 at the time of entry. The winner, if Canadian, will be required to answer correctly a time-limited arithmetical skill testing question in order to receive the prize. Employees of Bantam Doubleday Dell Publishing Group Inc. and its subsidiaries and affiliates and their immediate family members are not eligible. Void where prohibited or restricted by law. Grand and first prize winners will be required to execute and return within 14 days of notification an affidavit of eligibility and release to be signed by winner and winner's parent or legal guardian. In the event of noncompliance with this time period, an alternate winner will be chosen.
4. Entering the sweepstakes constitutes permission for use of the winner's name, likeness, and biographical data for publicity and promotional purposes on behalf of BDD, with no additional compensation. For the name of the winner, available after January 31, 1994, send a self-addressed envelope, entirely separate from your entry, to Bantam Doubleday Dell, BFYR Marketing Department, 1540 Broadway, New York, NY 10036.